Life, Love, Death, Debauchery
(not necessarily in that order)

A collection of 5 playlets

Debbie Nagioff

TSL Drama

First published in Great Britain in 2022
By TSL Publications, Rickmansworth

Copyright © 2022 Debbie Nagioff

ISBN: 978-1-915660-23-7

Cover courtesy of : pixabay

Life, Love, Death, Debauchery
(not necessarily in that order)

For

Rami & Daniel

The Foot of the Bed

Delia [who is referred to as Della] is desperately ill in hospital. At the foot of her bed are her deceased "grandparents" Bert and Reen who are in spirit and waiting for her to pass over so they can greet her on the other side and take her soul on its journey. When eventually Delia passes over, it becomes obvious that the grandparents are waiting at the wrong bed and there has been a clerical error. Add to that a sympathetic nurse, matter-of-fact doctor and Delia's real father [in spirit] and you have the ingredients for a comedy drama playlet with a difference.

Running time
10 mins

Cast

BERT	An elderly rather argumentative man – rather course in his manner. 80+ – London cockney accent
REEN	Elderly argumentative woman – warm hearted and well meaning. 80+ London cockney accent
DELLA/DELIA	Is referred to as Della but she turns out to be Delia. Late 50s or early 60s
NURSE	Dreamy, sensitive in her 20s
DOCTOR	Brash, young, 35-ish
ABE	Delia's father. 70s and very warm

DELLA *is desperately ill in hospital.* BERT *and* REEN *are sitting at the foot of her bed. We don't see* DELLA's *face, only her shape in bed. Her grandmother wears a coat and old fashioned hat. She has her handbag on her lap. Her grandfather wears a flat cap and has a cigarette behind his ear.*

"DELLA" *starts moaning and flailing around. But* BERT *and* REEN *look at her quite impassively.*

BERT: This is a bit of a drag ain't it, Reen? [*sighs*]

REEN: Oh Bert. Shut up.

BERT: Well I don't see the point of being here frankly. She's not, you know.

REEN: What?

BERT: Doing anything.

REEN: Don't worry. You'll see.

BERT: I could have watched the football.

REEN: What, twenty-two sods kicking a ball at the Emirates?

BERT: Yeah, well. [*looks around the hospital ward and then belches loudly*]. Pardon.

REEN: Must you?

BERT: Better up than down.

           [DELLA *starts to laugh.*]

DELLA: [*mumbling*] Up and down. Up and down. Up and down.

           [*A* DOCTOR *and* NURSE *fly to her side and start examining her.*]

NURSE: Did you hear her doctor?

DOCTOR: I'm not deaf, am I?

NURSE: Sorry.

BERT: These friggin' doctors.

REEN: Bert, shut up.

DELLA: [*mumbling*] Granddad.

BERT:	Sorry love. Slip of the tongue.
NURSE:	I think she's delirious.
BERT:	No, it's "Della".
REEN:	She's not interested in what you have to say.
BERT:	No respect for their elders.
REEN:	Doctor, is she alright?
DOCTOR:	[*to* NURSE] I'm not very happy about her. I don't think she'll last the night.
BERT:	[*mumbling*] Friggin' Aida!
REEN:	Doctor, can you do something?
BERT:	Thought you said he's not interested.
	[REEN *glares*]
DOCTOR:	Mmm. [*examining her*] Her pulse is very weak.
NURSE:	[*getting upset*] Oh no.
DOCTOR:	What?
NURSE:	I'm scared, doctor.
DOCTOR:	But you're a nurse for crying out loud.
NURSE:	I know.
DOCTOR:	Why on earth did you bother?
BERT:	I don't believe these two!!
REEN:	She's got a point, though.
NURSE:	I'm good at the "looking after" side, but not, you know...
DOCTOR:	I hope you're not going to get hysterical on me, because if you do, you'll be shown the door.
NURSE:	No of course not, doctor. Do you think she'll feel anything when she dies?
DOCTOR:	You're asking the wrong person.
NURSE:	[*looks upset*] Doctor, where do you think we go after we die?
DOCTOR:	To the hospital morgue.
NURSE:	Oh.

DOCTOR: As far as I'm concerned, once you're dead, you're dead.

NURSE: I think you're wrong.

DOCTOR: Nurse, I think we need to terminate this conversation.

REEN: Oh, for goodness' sake.

BERT: He's a little snot isn't he?

DOCTOR: Keep an eye on her. According to her notes we can resuscitate.

NURSE: Yes, doctor.

DOCTOR: And perhaps you'd better ask yourself why you became a nurse.

NURSE: Yes, doctor.

[DELLA *groans*]

REEN: Can you hear me love? It's grandma. We're here, love. Are you comfortable?

DELLA: Yes. Yes. Oh yes.

NURSE: What shall we do?

DOCTOR: Give her a sedative. You know how to do that, don't you?

NURSE: Yes, of course, I er...

DOCTOR: I'll do it. Just watch, okay?

BERT: Oh that's right, knock her out. Answer to everything, isn't it?

DOCTOR: It should knock her out.

BERT: I just said that. Didn't I just say that?

["DELLA" *starts to moan. The* DOCTOR *disappears and then returns.*]

REEN: Yeah, right. My husband, the doctor.

BERT: Yeah, well. I could have been.

REEN: No you couldn't.

BERT::   I could.

[DELLA *moans.* NURSE *arrives and gives her an injection.*]

BERT: There it goes. Right into her vein, in a few minutes she'll be as quiet as a mouse. Little love.

[*"DELLA" moans, but a phone rings and the* NURSE *goes to stage left to answer it. We can't hear the phone conversation. But we see she is still very distressed, but then starts to smile.* BERT *follows her to the phone.*]

REEN: Bert, come and sit down. It's not nice.

BERT: [*turning to* REEN] She's talking to her bloody boyfriend.

REEN: It's not our business. These nurses have got to have a life. Poor little cow.

BERT: Straight up, she is. Oi, what about our "Della"? You can talk to him later.

[*The* NURSE *smiles as she talks to the man on the phone, and starts preening herself*]

REEN: Come and sit down.

BERT: Yep. She'll get a good rogering later.

DELLA: Roger. Roger. Roger.

REEN: You see what you've started?

NURSE: She must be calling for her husband. [*she rushes to "DELLA"'s bed*]

NURSE: Did you say something?

BERT: You have to laugh, haven't you.

DELLA: Roger. Oh Roger.

BERT: Yeah that's right love.

REEN: Bert. Honestly.

NURSE: I'll get the doctor. [*pitching*] Doctor? Doctor?

DOCTOR: What's happening?

BERT: Here he comes. The dipstick.

NURSE: I don't know. She keeps talking about a Roger.

[DOCTOR *takes her pulse.*]

BERT: They always did that in the movies. What was that series in the sixties?

REEN: *Crossroads.*

BERT: No.

REEN: *Man from Uncle.*

BERT: No.

REEN: I know, *The Avengers.*

BERT: No, the doctor series with what's-his-face?

REEN: Sid James.

BERT: No. Richard somebody.

REEN: Oh, I know who you mean.

BERT: Who do I mean?

REEN: Richard O'Sullivan.

BERT: No.

REEN: Richard Curtis?

BERT: Not Richard Curtis. He was a kid in the '60s. That bloke with the hair.

REEN: Jill Browne?

BERT: Chamberlain. Richard Chamberlain.

REEN: What hair?

BERT: But he used to do that.

REEN: The blond hair?

BERT: You know. That "Emergency Ward 10" lark.

REEN: You're confusing me now. Raymond Burr.

BERT: No. No. That was *Chief Ironside.*

REEN: Full of himself he was.

REEN: [*pitching*] You alright our "Della"?

DELLA: I'm dying.

REEN: Doctor, nurse, come quick.

[NURSE *approaches*. DELLA *moans*.]

NURSE: Are you alright, love? It'll be alright.

DELLA: I can't... can't...

NURSE: Just relax. Just relax.

REEN: Okay. [*going into her handbag and talking to* BERT] Fancy a toffee?

BERT: No thanks. They'll do my teeth in.

           [*The* NURSE *exits*]

REEN: Oh, okay.

BERT::   Got any sherbets?

REEN: No. They're full of sugar, them.

BERT: Well what about them rhubarb and custard ones?

REEN: You finished them off.

BERT: Did I?

REEN: You had a pig out you did.

BERT: I was hungry. [*starts looking around*]
           They certainly keep these wards clean, don't they?

REEN: Well they have to.

BERT: Not like them army hospitals during the war. Tents they were. During the war...

REEN: Oh shut up.

           [BERT *starts picking his nose.*]

REEN: Must you.

BERT: What?

REEN: That!

BERT: I'm only rubbing it.

REEN: Yeah, right.

BERT: These wards are so bloody hot.

REEN: Well these people are all ill.

BERT: [*sarcastically*] Really? I hadn't noticed.

["DELLA" *starts moaning*]

REEN   Oh be quiet. You're giving me the right hump now. Stop fidgeting.

BERT: Well I'm bored. And there's no action.

REEN: Patience. Patience.

BERT: She might get well again.

REEN: She might.

BERT: And we'd have been on a wild goose chase.

[*"DELLA" starts thrashing around, coughing and starts to choke*]

BERT: [*calling*] 'Ere nurse? Over 'ere dear.

[*The* NURSE *comes straight over. She looks around as if she heard something. Shakes her head then starts dealing with* "DELLA" *but can't stabilise her.*]

NURSE: Doctor. Doctor. Quick.

[*The* DOCTOR *races over*]

BERT: Now that's better. You see. That's how she should react.

[*As the* DOCTOR *races over,* DELLA's *body goes floppy. There is silence.*

Pause.]

BERT: Is that it?

REEN: Shh. Wait.

[*The* DOCTOR *puts his stethoscope on to* "DELLA", *then puts his head close to her mouth and then to her chest*]

BERT: Come on man? Don't keep us in suspenders?

REEN: Not suspenders, you daft brush.

BERT: I remember when you wore suspenders.

REEN: Yeah, well I was young and foolish.

BERT: And a right little cracker.

REEN: Yeah, well. That's until my dad found out.

BERT: Yeah, he weren't too happy. [*shooting an imaginary shot gun*]

DOCTOR: Her pulse is very faint, nurse.

NURSE: Okay, doctor. I'll watch her.

DOCTOR: Let me know if there's any change.

BERT: Oi, I need some change for the coffee machine.

REEN: You don't need coffee.

BERT: Don't tell me what I need.

[*The* NURSE *and* DOCTOR *walk away*]

BERT: Well I think the show's over.

REEN: 'Ere Bert, do you think we should have brought grapes with us. Or flowers?

BERT: What for?

REEN: I don't know. I thought it would be nice when she comes round kind of thing.

BERT: Well that may take time.

["DELLA"s *arm drops to the side. She has died.*]

REEN: I think she's gone, Bert.

BERT: Yep. Show time.

REEN: [*getting up*] Nurse? Nurse?

BERT: Don't be daft, Reen.

REEN: Oh, I forgot.

[*The* NURSE *runs to* "DELLA", *again looking around as if she heard something. The* DOCTOR *follows. They pull the curtains round her, but* BERT *and* REEN *are still in view.*]

REEN: What do you think they're doing?

BERT: [*he pulls the curtain back slightly*] Panicking. [*he looks at his watch*] Shouldn't be too long now.

[*The* DOCTOR *and* NURSE *come from behind the curtain.*]

DOCTOR: [*matter of factly*] Nothing that we could have done. We'll get this organised.

BERT:	You haven't got Dr Kildare's bedside manner.
REEN:	He's too young to remember that.
NURSE:	Okay doctor.
DOCTOR:	Cheer up. You better get on to, Roger was it?
NURSE:	I'll check the file.
	[*The* DOCTOR *and* NURSE *move off stage*]
BERT:	Oh Gawd!
REEN:	The kids will be heartbroken. Such a shame.
BERT:	Yep. What can you do, that's life.
REEN:	Yeah.
BERT:	I remember seeing my dear parents die. Bless 'em.
REEN:	How are they?
BERT:	Not bad. Dad's very into his music these days. Attends a lot of concerts. Mum's taken up a theological degree.
REEN:	That's good.
BERT:	What seems to be keeping her then? Can't get her bum out of bed?
REEN:	Patience.
BERT:	I think I hear a stirring. 5-4-3-2-1
	[*The spirit of* "DELLA" *comes out from behind the curtain. Her face is white. Her arms are by her side.*]
BERT:	Hello love.
REEN:	Hello darling. You'll be fine now.
DELLA:	Who are you?
BERT:	It's granddad, pet. Don't you remember? It's been a long time?
DELLA:	Must have been.
BERT:	When you was little.
REEN:	I know we've changed a lot, pet. We've come to take you onwards.

DELLA: Where?

BERT: To heaven.

DELLA: What are you talking about?

REEN: To the next world. You're dead "Della". Deceased. Gone. Finished.

DELLA: Della? I'm not Della. I'm Delia.

REEN: Delia?

BERT: Delicious more like.

REEN: Bert, shut up, this is your fault.

DELIA: I'm sorry to put you to all this bother.

REEN: Oh it's no bother, pet. Bert, how did this happen?

BERT: I don't know. Wait a minute.

           [BERT *takes out piece of paper from his pocket and reads it.*]

BERT: Doesn't that say "Della on Ward 10" to you?

REEN: [*takes out reading glasses*] It's "Della on Ward 16" you pillock!

BERT::   Bloody hell.

DELIA: Excuse me...

BERT: Can't be. Now that's not my fault, is that. Do you see how they've written it? That is never a "6".

REEN: Well, check the notes at the bottom of the bed if you want to be sure.

BERT: Alright, alright, keep your wig on. There's a perfectly reasonable explanation.

DELIA: Excuse me...

REEN: Bert, you aren't listening to me.

DELIA: Excuse me...

REEN: Will you check the notes or shall I?

           [BERT *looks at the notes but is straining*]

BERT:	I haven't got me glasses. [*peering*] Hang on. [*reading slowly*] Delia Berkowitz! [*stumbling over the name*] It's the wrong friggin' bed!
REEN:	Typical.
DELIA:	Can you tell me what I should do?
REEN:	Just a minute, love.
BERT:	We knew the Berkowitzes. Abe Berkowitz?
REEN:	Wasn't there a Berkowitz in Cable Street?
BERT:	Nah, those were the Bermans.
DELIA:	That's it. My Dad was Abe Berkowitz.
BERT:	Nice bloke was Abe. He always got the best conkers.
REEN:	The Bermans didn't live in Cable Street. They lived in New Road. Your memory drives me mad.
DELIA:	They were in Whitechapel Road, actually.
BERT:	What about your memory?
REEN:	I don't have one.
BERT:	So Delia, we'll wait till Dad arrives. It'll be nice to see Abe again. Might be able to get even with him on the old conker front.
DELIA:	Oh thank you. Do you think he'll come? Do you think he'll be long?
BERT:	Long? He was late for his own funeral.
DELIA:	It's very kind of you to wait with me.
BERT:	Don't mention it. Sorry for the balls up.
REEN:	Bert, language!
BERT:	Sorry. I'm sure Abe will come along for you in a minute, then we'll have to go and find our Della.
DELIA:	But what shall I do? I'm stuck between two worlds here.
BERT:	There might be an old magazine lying around in Casualty? What's today?
REEN:	Monday.

BERT:	Well, I've heard *The Times* crossword is a bit hard going of a Monday. Not that I've ever done it, mind. 'Ere, you're a bit of alright actually.
REEN:	Bert. Leave her along. She's dead.
BERT:	Sorry. It's been a long time!
DELIA:	I wish you wouldn't keep saying I'm dead.
REEN:	Sorry. He's a randy old prat. You're not dead. You're an angel. Now we have to go. Bert, I think it's Apple Ward we want. We'll have to hurry.
DELIA:	Does that mean you won't take me?
REEN:	Oh, come on then. [*pause*] Wait a minute. Look who's here.
	[*Enter* DELIA's FATHER. *He's wearing an old fashioned cap and has a piece of paper in his hand. He sees* BERT *and* REEN. DELIA *turns to him. They look at each other, he looks at* ???]
DELIA:	Daddy?
ABE:	Delia? My little princess. Sorry, I went to the wrong bed. [*looking at the piece of paper*] It said, "Delia on Ward 16". But the writing is bad. Wait a minute, Bert? Is that you?
BERT:	Yeah. Nice seeing you Abe. You alright?
ABE:	Not bad. You know. Up and down.
BERT:	Yeah, I know the feeling. Anyhow. She's all yours.
ABE:	Ta, Bert for looking after her. Reen. You okay? It's been a long time since Cable Street. I saw your mother the other day.
REEN:	Really? She's looking good, no?
ABE:	Yep. But very argumentative.
BERT:	'Ere Abe, you still got that prize cheeser?
ABE:	Funny you should mention that. [*pulling a conker on a string from under his cap*] Ready?
BERT:	Ready.
	[ABE *throws his cap on the floor and* BERT *pulls out a conker from his pocket also on a string and they begin a conker fight. They enjoy themselves.*]

REEN:	Bert.
BERT:	Just a minute.
REEN:	Bert. We've work to do.
BERT:	Oh yeah, that's right. I've gotta go Abe. It's been fun. Here's your daughter.
	[*They shake hands*]
ABE:	Yeah. Thanks for looking after her.
BERT:	See you Abe. Reen. Cloud 9?
ABE:	Yeah. Cloud 9! And the conker challenge still stands.
BERT:	You bet!
	[BERT *and* REEN *look for a brief moment, smile and move off.* ABE *starts looking at his daughter.*]
ABE:	Delia?
DELIA:	Daddy. [*she starts to cry*] I've been waiting for you.
ABE:	I know. I'm sorry. I got lost.
DELIA:	Got lost? But you're a cabbie!
ABE:	Not much of one then! And not much of a dad either. I never was. That's what Mum used to say.
DELIA:	It doesn't matter, anymore.
ABE:	Remember when I lost you when we went up West?
DELIA:	It's fine. I loved you anyway. Come here.
	[ABE *steps forward*]
DELIA:	You look so young. [*she starts touching his face*] And so perfect.
ABE:	I'm not in pain any more.
DELIA:	Oh, I'm glad. [*she starts to cry*] How do I look?
ABE:	My little baby girl.
DELIA:	I'm a 60 year old woman.
ABE:	Look down at yourself.
	[DELIA *looks down at herself*]

ABE: You're young again. So perfect. Just as you always were.

DELIA: You're so handsome.

ABE: Give your dad a big hug.

            [*Just before they embrace he chucks the conker onto the floor. They embrace.*]

DELIA: I've missed you.

ABE: And I, you. Come on. I'm taking you onward.

DELIA: Daddy?

ABE: Yes my pet?

DELIA: Nothing.

            [*They go.*

            Pause.

            Enter DOCTOR *in a general hurry. He looks around the ward. He stumbles over the conker and the cap. He grimaces. Picks the cap up, tries it on, and then at a swanky angle. Shrugs, takes off the cap puts it and the conker on the bed.*]

DOCTOR: Nurse. This patient needs a clean up.

            [*The* NURSE *comes in. She opens a window and looks at the body of* DELIA. *We can't see her as it's just a lump in the bed.*]

NURSE: [*to the body of* DELIA] So peaceful. I need to wash you now Delia to make you fresh for your family. Oh, I've forgotten the bowl, silly me. I'll be back in a minute.

            [*As she is about to leave, she sees the cap on the bed with the conker.*]

NURSE: How did these get here?

She picks them up and looks at them, and then looks thoughtfully into the distance as if she is trying to understand where they've come from.

Suddenly ABE *and* DELIA *re-appear.* DELIA *wants to say goodbye. The* NURSE *sees her and gasps.* DELIA *gives a gentle wave. The* NURSE *looks away briefly and at the lump in the bed. When she looks back,* DELIA *and* ABE *have gone.*

The Last Sunrise

CAST

[In order of appearance]

Ben Jacobs	in his 70s
Dr Smythe	Psychiatrist – 30s to 40s
Ben Jacobs	as a young boy – 13
Isaac Jacobs	[Ben's father] Early 30s
Rosetta Jacobs	[Ben's mother] Late 20s [she also sings at end and beginning]
Miriam Jacobs	about 10
Female Voice	30s
Male Guard	20s

Running Time

6 minutes

Song before first scene lights up

[sung in waltz timing by Rosetta Jacobs]

> *Shteyt a bocher, shteyt un tracht,*
> *tracht un tracht a gantze nacht.*
> *Vemen tsu nemen un nit far shemen,*
> *vemen tsu nemen un nit far shemen*

Psychiatrist's Office and Events in Nazi Germany

The stage is split into two. When one side is active, the other is in darkness.

BEN JACOBS *is in his 70s. He's sitting in the couch opposite his psychiatrist* DR SMYTHE.

BEN: Oh no. I hear that song again.

SMYTHE: The one you told me about last time?

BEN: Yes. It was Mama's favourite. [*starts singing in a disjointed way*] "Tumbala, tumbala, tumbalalaika".

SMYTHE: So, Ben. If we're to get to the root of all these nightmares you've been having, you must tell me everything that happened in those years.

BEN: I can't. I can't remember.

SMYTHE: Take your time. Take your time. [*looks at his watch.*]

BEN: We had been 16 months in a camp in Theresienstadt. Then one day we heard we were to be sent to Auschwitz. [*shaking with emotion*]

SMYTHE: Go on.

BEN: We were pushed onto a train. It had cattle cars. We were herded in like animals. There was pandemonium everywhere – moaning, crying, screaming.

Black out and light up on War Events part of stage

BEN (13):   Papa, where are we going?

ISAAC: I don't know, son. Let it be an adventure.

ROSETTA: Don't be afraid, Ben, we're altogether.

MIRIAM:	You look scared Mama. Where are we going?
ROSETTA:	It'll be alright.
BEN:	Why are all these people screaming?
VOICE:	[*shouting*] Tell your children the truth Rosetta Jacobs. We're all going to Auschwitz and we're all going to be gassed. [*she starts crying*]
BEN (13):	Gassed? What does she mean, Mama?
ISAAC:	[*moaning and groaning*] Oh my stomach, quick, help me before it's too late.
ROSETTA:	Isaac! Isaac!

Black out and light up the PSYCHIATRIST's *room*

BEN:	I had to watch how my big, strong Papa, my hero, let down his trousers and without shame, sat on the shit bucket in front of all these people. It was a defining moment for me.
SMYTHE:	What happened next?

Black out. Light up War events

VOICE:	I think we can get this barbed wire loose. Come on if everyone tries, we can do it.
ISAAC:	But we'll be shot at.
VOICE:	We've got to try and get out, after the stench you left.
ISAAC:	It's not my fault.
ROSETTA:	Isaac, don't fight.
ISAAC:	Okay, you're right. Maybe we can make a run for it.
ROSETTA:	But there's SS on the roof.
VOICE:	I need your help Isaac Jacobs.
ISAAC:	I'm doing my best.
VOICE:	My fingers are raw. Come on. Come on.
ISAAC:	I'm working as fast as I can.
VOICE:	I think it's coming away, the barbed wire is coming away. Come on everyone, get off this death train.
ISAAC:	Rosetta, you take the children.

ROSETTA: But I don't want to leave you.

ISAAC: Go. Go. If there's a God in heaven, we shall be together again, all of us.

BEN (13): I'm going to stay with you, Papa.

ISAAC: Go. Go with your mother. It's now or never.

ROSETTA: Come on, Ben. Come on.

MIRIAM: Mama, I can't leave Papa and Ben.

ROSETTA: You will do as you're told.

Black out. Light up PSYCHIATRIST's *office*

BEN: And so Mama and Miriam jumped, along with others from our train. And as they jumped, Papa and I heard rapid gun fire. They were dead before their bodies touched the soft snow. But at least they were free. The train stopped for a moment. There was an uneasy silence. Each corpse was attached to a long rivulet of crimson blood that left a pink tinge on the snow. I was in shock, but riveted, fascinated and mesmerized all in one go. I thought I saw a flicker of a smile on my mother's lifeless face. She looked so serene, as if she had been united with the Light.

SMYTHE: And what happened to you and your Papa.

BEN: Days later we arrived at Auschwitz. We were stripped, shaved and made to walk naked in a line that wended its way slowly towards a smoking building. It was the first time I'd seen naked women. They were trying to cover themselves, their shame. Despite the screams of the dying coming from this building, we could hear an orchestra playing.

Black out. Fade up War scenes

BEN (13): Papa, I'm so cold.

ISAAC: Don't worry, I will keep you warm my son. [*he puts arm around his son*] And we will see mummy soon and Miriam.

BEN (13): What do you mean?

ISAAC: You'll see.

BEN (13):   But dad, they're dead.

ISAAC: No. No. Not dead. They escaped, and I know they're alive somewhere. It would have been too cold for them to lay on the snow. Listen to that lovely music, Ben.

BEN (13):   Where is it coming from?

ISAAC: From the concert hall. Look ahead of you. It's a concert hall. You can hear the music, can't you? It's Bach, I think.

Fade to black. Fade up PSYCHIATRIST's *chair.*

BEN: The "concert hall", with its stench of rotting flesh billowing out into the sky, was looming ever closer.

Fade to black. Fade up War events.

ISAAC: How are you feeling, Ben? Are you excited?

BEN (13):   About what?

ISAAC: The concert. We're all going to a concert.

BEN (13):   But Papa, we're naked. Nobody goes naked to the opera or the ballet.

ISAAC: There's a first time for everything you know. Mummy would love it. We must embrace the new Germany and its values. Hitler is right. We are filth. That's why we are being cleansed before we hear the beautiful music.

BEN (13):   Papa, what are you talking about?

              [*The music gets louder and louder*]

ISAAC: Tumbala, tumbala, tumbalalaika,
              Tumbala, tumbala, tumbalalaika,
              tumbalalaika, shpiel balalaika
              tumbalalaika – freylach zol zayn

BEN (13):   Papa?

ISAAC: Your mama used to sing that to you, when you were little. Do you remember? Such a little boy you were. I'm sure she'd sing that to you again if you wanted. Just because you're 13 and a man, doesn't mean we can't bend the rules a little for a barmitzvah boy.

GUARD: Stop please.

           [*By now the music has got very loud*]

ISAAC: [*shouting*] Oh my God. Oh my God.

GUARD: Stop. Who are you, please?

ISAAC   I... I... I'm Isaac Jacobs and I'm a tailor, a very good tailor. That's a very fine uniform you're wearing. Perhaps I could stitch that button on tighter for you if you like. Oh, and this is my beautiful son Ben. You won't hurt him, will you?

GUARD: Go inside old man. We don't need your expertise anymore. You've used up your last cotton reel. [*laughs*] But your beautiful son, he can be of use to us.

BEN (13): But I want my papa.

GUARD: Stand aside, boy.

ISAAC: Can I just speak to him? Can I just speak to my beautiful son one last time?

GUARD: No.

BEN (13): Please Papa, don't argue with him.

ISAAC: [*disappearing*] My Ben. My beautiful son, remember to say kaddish for me.

           [ISAAC *is kicked violently and falls down*]

ISAAC: Aah!

GUARD: Get up, old man before I stamp on your fingers and break them.

ISAAC: [*agonized*] Wait. I'm doing it. Don't hit me. Don't hit me.

GUARD: I warned you.

ISAAC: [*let's out a scream*] My fingers. My fingers.

GUARD: You Jews! Go and fester in the next world.

BEN (13): Papa! Papa!

The War Events side of the stage freezes. The lights are still up on that side of the stage. Slow fade up of the psychiatric chair.

SMYTHE: So, you were taken away?

BEN: I never saw my daddy again. I was taken away, clothed and put to work. A year later we were liberated and I lived a nomadic existence till eventually I met Rosa, my wife. But my family was lost to me forever.

SMYTHE: And then?

BEN: [*long pause*] And then.

Tumbala, tumbala, tumbalalaika,
Tumbala, tumbala, tumbalalaika

We see BEN's *mother,* ROSETTA *walking across the set and joining him in the song.*

ROSETTA: tumbalalaika, shpiel balalaika
tumbalalaika - freylach zol zayn

[*starts humming*]

BEN: Mama? Mama? [*his breathing becomes very rapid and difficult*]

ROSETTA: My sweet baby boy.

[*starts stroking his face*]

BEN: Mama. Wait for me. I can't lose you a second time.

BLACK OUT

SMYTHE: Ben? Ben? Wake up.

Pride & Strine

CAST

FINN   Broad Australian actor, who can sing opera, but
                doesn't understand Jane Austin, playing Fitzwilliam
                Darcy – Early 30s.

CHARLENE   Broad Australian actress playing Miss Elizabeth
                Bennett. She tries to sustain a haughty English
                accent, but it all goes south in the end – Early 20s

BAZZA   An over exuberant director – Mid 30s.

WOMAN on beach Mid 30s.

Running Time

7 minutes

Rehearsal room of the Wonga Wonga Light Operatic Drama Group

The Wonga Wonga Light Operatic Drama Group, in New South Wales, Australia, are rehearsing their own rendition of the proposal scene between Mr Darcy and Elizabeth Bennett from Pride & Prejudice. *But they are aiming for a completely revolutionary and locally acceptable version.*

FINN, *who is playing Darcy, is practising a musical number from the show.* CHARLENE *is playing Miss Elizabeth Bennett.* BAZZA, *the director watches the rehearsal unfold.*

FINN:
[*operatically and to the tune of "Summertime and the living is easy"*]

Dinnertime, and I've heard she is easy
My jock is jumpin'
And her bosoms are high.

You know I'm rich
And I'm very good lookin

So shut your face baby
And know the reason why

[*he takes the last note high and his voice cracks and breaks into a broad Australian accent*]

Oh Jeez, I can't get that damn note!

BAZZA:
Well, no worries Finn. Let's just run the scene as we've been practising it, huh?

FINN:
Yep. I've really gotta get into this in the only way I know how. And it begins with the strides for me! Darcy was a guy with a button fly. Not a zipper sort of a bloke. So he was very, very pedantic.

BAZZA:
Whatever works for you, mate. But just remember we're on the beach for this scene. Elizabeth Bennett is sitting under a large umbrella, in her bikini, when Darcy strolls over to her with his surf board and a sock stuffed down his lycras.

FINN:
So, shall I embrace the sock?

BAZZA:
Whatever works for you. So, let's take it from the top.

FINN:
Okay.

BAZZA: And... approach her.

FINN: Goodday Liz. Jeezus, these shorts are cutting me groin to the quick. Anyways for a long time now Liz, I've felt me juices, you know, kinda pumping around and bubbling below the surface? And I can't hold 'em no longer. They're going to spill any minute now. So how's about naming the day.

CHARLENE: In such a case as this, I believe the right response would be to give you a kick up the jacksy, and to express a sense obligation. But don't get too cocky. I have never desired your good opinion.

FINN: Oh. Strewth girl, give a guy a break. I know I had a few beers down on the beach last night [*belches*] excuse I, [*sniffing himself*] And I smell worse than a kangaroo's fart, but, I'm a good sort of bloke and a bloody good surfer. Ask me mum. Besides, you won't do better than me. A stuck up bird such as yourself. [*belches*] Them tarts on the beach thinking I'm bloody fit!

CHARLENE: Is that so? I might as well ask why you want to bother with me, with so evident a design of offending and insulting me. What's the point?

And why be so uncouth about it? Now move away, you're blocking my sun.

FINN: Oh, sorry. Do you know where the nearest dunny is?

CHARLENE: Wait till the end of the play. Oh, and by the way, that dippy friend of yours...

FINN: Who? Charlie Bingley?

CHARLENE: That's the guy; did you talk him into splitting up with our Jane, and ruining, perhaps for ever, her happiness and hope of marrying a rich bastard, although not so rich as you?

FINN: Abso- fucking- lutely. I'm a jealous sort of bloke with a poker up me arse, and I hate seeing people so bloody happy. So I told Chazza a few porkies, and Bob's your uncle, he dumped her.

CHARLENE: So you don't even have the nouce to deny it?

FINN: What's nouce?

CHARLENE: You know, thingy!

FINN: Oh right. Whatever.

CHARLENE: I have every reason in the world to think that marrying you would be the biggest mistake of my life. You're ungenerous...

FINN: I'll buy you a coke.

CHARLENE: No thanks. And, getting back to what I was saying, do you deny that you separated them?

FINN: I told you before, you cloth-eared bint. I did it. I bloody did it. Weren't you listening? Sorry, Baz, do we need to repeat that?

BAZZA: Leave it in for the time being.

FINN: Okay. You're the boss.

CHARLENE: I am listening, Mr Darcy and you're still blocking my sun.

FINN: Oh sorry, sorry.

CHARLENE: But it's not only because of this that I hate your guts.

FINN: Strewth! Don't you go on and on and on.

CHARLENE: I realised what a jealous pig you were when you started pulling faces and sticking yer tongue out at me, when I was being touched up, I mean chatted up by Mr Wickham. What have you got to say about that?

FINN: Well you was all over him like a rash.

CHARLENE: You don't say "you was", that's very common. It's "you were".

FINN: They won't notice in Wonga Wonga.

CHARLENE: But you're forgetting sir, you were supposedly bred in one of the finest houses in Derbyshire.

FINN: What do you want with that wanker, Wickham?

CHARLENE: Wanker? I don't think so sir. If anyone's a wanker, it's you, with that ridiculous sock stuffed down your kacks!

            [*Pulling the sock out and throwing it over his shoulder. It lands on top of an unsuspecting woman on the beach.*]

FINN: There, it's gone.

WOMAN ON BEACH: Hey! What're you doing?

FINN: Sorry madam, I was just trying to get me leg over. I mean I was proposing to one of the most beautiful wenches in Hertfordshire.

WOMAN ON THE BEACH: That must be Miss Elizabeth Bennett, whose eyes, we are all led to believe, are very fine.

FINN: Really? They look a bit squinty to me, but that may be the sun. So, Liz, what about that Wickham? The lucky bastard. You seem to take a keen interest in him.

CHARLENE: Lucky? I think he's been most unlucky.

FINN: Oh yeah? Why's that?

CHARLENE: I don't know actually. Sorry can we just break? Bazza, why is Wickham saying he's so unfortunate?

BAZZA: Ah, because he's crap with money, and spends it all on women.

CHARLENE: Oh, okay. Then why would I be interested in him?

BAZZA: Because after that duffer, Mr Collins, anyone looks great.

CHARLENE: Right. Right. That works for me. Okay. Sorry. You could have helped him out. But you were as tight as a tick. You have deprived him of the best years of his life of independence which he deserved, and now he wanders aimlessly trying to find an anchor. You have done all this! And yet you can treat the mention of his bad luck with contempt and ridicule.

FINN: Now hold on sister. This is your opinion of me! This is what you think? Well ta for letting me know. I must be a right twat and my faults, according to you, are heavy indeed!

But you're a proud sort of Sheila, and I've heard you bang better than a shit-house door in a storm.

Maybe if I'd dressed up with long sideburns and a tail coat thingy, and brought you a few lamb chops from the barbie, these little observations might have been overlooked.

Maybe I should have flattered you and told you that you were a fair looking Sheila. But, frankly that ain't my style. Mind if I join you in that deckchair?

CHARLENE: No, please don't. And by the way You are mistaken, Mr. Darcy. It's not what you said, it's the way that you said it. Remember at that dance we all went to, you didn't even bother asking me for one [pause] or even a dance. So why pick on me now. I'm not impressed by your glitz and your money. How much are you worth by the way?

FINN: About $50 billion.

CHARLENE: $50 billion!!!!! Well, I might have been a bit hasty. But no, no, there's no turning back. You should have behaved in a more gentleman-like manner.

You could not have made me the offer of your hand or any other part of your body for that matter, in any possible way that would have tempted me to accept it.

FINN: Blah blah blah.

CHARLENE: You're just an arrogant and conceited sod with a selfish disdain of the feelings of others and a cheap aftershave.

FINN: Yep, yep, yep.

CHARLENE: And summarising...

FINN: Oh thank Christ.

CHARLENE: I feel that you are the last man in the world whom I could ever be prevailed on to marry. But I may change my mind if I saw your famous grounds at Wembley.

FINN: No, no. That's Pemberley, Charlene.

CHARLENE: Is it? I'll change that on the script.

FINN: Sorry, that's not on offer you grabbing little harpy.

CHARLENE: Harpy?

FINN: Yeah. You've said an awful lot, my chickadee. And I get it. And now I feel a prize prat for having spilled the beans on my feelings for you. Now, if you'll excuse me, I'm going to piss off and try the same line on some other bird, as I'm getting pretty desperate here! [*adjusts his shorts*]

CHARLENE: You do that.

[FINN *walks off*]

CHARLENE: [*to herself*] 50 billion dollars though. That's like music. 50 billion dollars. My family could move out of that frankly very naff rundown house of theirs, and move up North. [*calls after* DARCY] Hey Darcy, Darcy, yoo hoo. I've changed me mind.

END

Mullered!

CAST

EDDIE ["Ed"]	Television Director
SUSIE	Transmission Assistant
JEFFO	Male Floor Manager
CAMERA 1	Male or female
CAMERA 2	Male or female
CAMERA 3	Male or female
DIANA	Chat show hostess
FIONA YENTA	Actress
DENISE VAN SCHTUPP	Actress

Running Time
5 minutes

Note to Actors: DIANA, FIONA *and* DENISE *should stand together to stage right.* REST OF THE CAST *should stand together stage left.*

Television Gallery /Live Studio of A Chat Show

EDDIE: Okay is everybody ready? Susie?

SUSIE: Yep.

EDDIE: Jeffo? [*pause*] Jeffo, can you hear me?

JEFFO: [*through talkback*] Yes Eddie.

EDDIE: Is she okay today?

JEFFO: Mmm, well ...

EDDIE: Too late! Cameras?

3 CAMERAs: Yes Eddie?

EDDIE: Okay.

SUSIE: Okay, ten to go [*starts counting down from ten over next speeches*] 10-9-8-7-6

EDDIE: Camera 1, let's have a close up on Diana.

SUSIE: 5-4-3-2-1

EDDIE: Cue Diana.

            [*cut into television studio. – music –*]

DIANA: Hello! And welcome to the show.

EDDIE: She seems okay to me. Go in closer Camera 1.

JEFFO: Yeah, maybe.

DIANA: I have two great guests this evening, Fiona Yenta who has been nominated for a BAFTA for her part as the love interest in "Drek"....I'm sorry, "Beck". And here she is.

            [*Applause from* CAST

            Enter FIONA YENTA]

DIANA: Hi Fiona. You look gorgeous.

FIONA: Hi Diana. Shall I sit here?

EDDIE: So far so good.

DIANA: Sit wherever you like, darling.

FIONA: Here?

DIANA: No, not there. That's reserved for our other BAFTA nominee, Denise van Schtupp. She's a very important guest you know.

JEFFO: Bugger.

FIONA: Oh. And I'm not?

DIANA: Of course you are darling.

EDDIE: Oh God. What did you put in her glass, Jeffo?

JEFFO: Ginger ale.

EDDIE: I don't think so.

DIANA: And next we have our other wonderful guest, Denise van Schtupp!

[CAST *applause*

Enter DENISE *heavily pregnant*]

DIANA: [*shocked*] My goodness Denise, how are you?

DENISE: As you can see, I'm in my third trimester.

DIANA: What number is this little cherub?

DENISE: Number four. I already have three boys.

DIANA: Four? Four? Are your legs in different post codes?

DENISE: Excuse me?

[FIONA *laughs*]

EDDIE: Shit!

[DIANA *laughs*]

JEFFO: It was definitely Ginger Ale, Eddie!

EDDIE: Camera 2, hold the mid-shot. Camera 3 dolly round.

DIANA: Anyway, I gather you two know each other.

FIONA: Yes, yes we do.

DENISE: [*coldly*] Oh you better believe it.

DIANA: Do I sense a little tension?

FIONA: Not from me.

DIANA: Good, good. So Fiona, tell us about your role in "Drek".

FIONA: It's "Beck".

DIANA: Sorry. I must have a word with our researcher.

EDDIE: It's "Beck", Diana, "Beck".

DIANA: Who said that? I'm hearing voices in my ear!

FIONA: Pardon?

DIANA: I'm very psychic you know. Oh, it's my director.

EDDIE: Shut up and focus Diana!

DIANA: He's having it off with our assistant, Susie.

SUSIE: Did you tell everybody, Eddie?

CAMERA 1: That's news to the crew.

CAMERA 2: Sure is. Wey-hey!

EDDIE: Shut up the lot of you. My wife is in the audience.

DIANA: So Fi!

FIONA: It's Fiona, actually!

DIANA: Whatever. Tell us about "Beck" and how you feel about your nomination.

FIONA: Well, "Beck" is about a female astronaut called Sylvie Beck who...

DIANA: [tapping her glass and loud whisper] Top up Jeffo.

JEFFO: Okay.

FIONA: Oh.

[JEFFO tops up her glass]

DIANA: Thanks. Sorry, sorry, Fiona, tell us about "Beck".

EDDIE: Oh my God.

FIONA: I was saying that "Beck" is about a female astronaut ...

DIANA: Yep, yep, yep, yep.

FIONA: ... called Sylvie, who makes it her life mission to become an astronaut despite her terrible past.

DIANA:	And Denise where did you get your terrible surname. I mean "Van Schtupp" – Per-leeze!
EDDIE:	Ah-oh!
FIONA:	Hang on, aren't you going to ask me more about "Drek", I mean "Beck".
DIANA:	Nah, not really.
EDDIE:	What she gonna say, Jeffo?
JEFFO:	How should I know?
DIANA:	Sounds like another shit movie with the usual overuse of the "green screen" and flimsy plot line.
FIONA:	I'm speechless.
DIANA:	Good. Now Denise, you're in a remake of *Pride & Prejudice* playing Lizzie Bennett. Did you get to shag D'Arcy in real life?
DENISE:	No I did not!
FIONA:	That's not what I heard.
DENISE:	I beg your pardon.
DIANA:	Just how did you get the part of Lizzie? Because, frankly looking at you…
EDDIE:	Can we go to commercial?
SUSIE:	This is the Beeb, Ed.
EDDIE:	Fuck!
DIANA:	… you're better off playing the barouche box.
	[FIONA *laughs*]
DENISE:	I don't think I like your tone.
FIONA:	I think she's got something there, Denise.
DENISE:	Has she now! Marriage wrecker!
FIONA:	I am not.
DENISE:	That's not what I heard.
DIANA:	Can I interject here?
FIONA/DENISE:	No.

FIONA:	Are you going to tell everybody whose baby you're carrying?
DENISE:	My husband's.
FIONA:	Oh the girl deserves the BAFTA straight off there... for lying.
DENISE:	I am not lying.
DIANA:	Another top up Jeffo?
JEFFO:	Er...
EDDIE:	Don't do it.
JEFFO:	[*loud whisper*] Eddie says no, Di.
DIANA:	What?
FIONA:	There is absolutely nothing about you that is genuine.
EDDIE:	What do I do?
SUSIE:	Ride it out, arse hole.
CAMERA 1:	This is better than the usual show.
DENISE;	What about you? False hair, false eyelashes... gastric band.
FIONA:	Your bulimia, beard, bad breath...
EDDIE:	Just keep them in mid-shot. Camera 3, what are you doing? And don't call me an arse hole.
SUSIE:	We're through!
CAMERA 3:	I think I need a pee.
EDDIE:	Too bad.
DIANA:	Girls, girls, this is my show and I need to bring some order into the proceedings.
EDDIE:	Oh, thank God. Relax everybody.
DIANA:	Denise, is there any truth to the rumour about your cocaine habit?
SUSIE:	Hey arse hole, there's a call for you on line 1.
EDDIE:	I'll take it.
DENISE:	No there isn't Diana. That was a false rumour put about by that bimbo sitting opposite me.

DIANA:	Oh, you mean Fiona.
DENISE:	Yes.
DIANA:	Well, none of us is perfect.
EDDIE:	Hi Dicky, what do you want us to do? Go to black? Really? But we'll be short by 25 minutes... You'll play music.
FIONA:	I'm going to tear your extensions out by the roots.
DENISE:	Go on then.
	[FIONA *and* DENISE *start fighting*]
DIANA:	Go on, give her a good slap, the slapper. Nobody comes on my show and behaves like that. Go on... get in there. Can we have a close up of the panti-less pregnant woman?
EDDIE:	Crew, we're going to black out. Start counting.
SUSIE:	Don't tell me what to do.
EDDIE:	I'll buy you a new Porsche and leave my wife. Okay?
SUSIE:	Ten to go, 9-8-7-6 [*continues to zero over next speeches*]
DIANA:	Jeffo, got any more of that amber nectar?
JEFFO:	You've finished the bottle.
EDDIE:	Thanks everybody! They've gone!
DIANA:	Eddie? Eddie? Hello? Are we still on air? The audience are leaving and they're still fighting.
EDDIE:	No, we are not on air.
DIANA:	What should I do? Girls! Girls!
DENISE:	I never slept with anyone but my husband and that is the honest truth. As God is my witness.
FIONA:	Oh, oh, Scarlett O'Hara.
DENISE:	Hang on. Hang on. Are we still on air?
DIANA:	No way.
FIONA:	Oh.
DENISE:	Oh. So, we may as well stop then.
DIANA:	Yeah.

EDDIE: Ladies, we're off the air. Goodnight! And you nearly got me fired.

FIONA: Shall we go over to the club for a drink then?

DENISE: Yeah.

DIANA: Great idea.

DENISE: I thought you were great in "Beck".

FIONA: And I thought your "Lizzie Bennett" was amazing. I'm so jealous!

DENISE: Friends again?

FIONA: Friends!

           [THEY *hug*]

DIANA: Come on girls, let's get mullered!

END

Into The Trench Via the Breach

CAST

Miss BREEZE	A teacher [Mid-30s]
Miss STEIN	A teacher [Mid-30s]
RYAN	Schoolboy aged 12
JOSH	Schoolboy aged 12
DANIEL	Schoolboy aged 12
JESSICA	Schoolgirl aged 12
SECURITY GUARD/HENRY V	
SOLDIER 1	Agincourt and World War 1
SOLDIER 2	Agincourt and World War 1
SOLDIER 3	Agincourt and World War 1
SOLDIER 4	World War 1

Running Time

11 minutes

Art Gallery

A class of 12 year olds and their teachers are walking round an Art Gallery. Some of the class are bored.

MISS BREEZE:	Can I have your attention please?
ALL:	Yes Miss Breeze.
MISS BREEZE:	I want you to look at this painting of The Battle of Agincourt?
RYAN:	I can paint better than that.
MISS BREEZE:	Ryan!
RYAN:	Well I can.
MISS BREEZE:	It will help you understand more fully Henry V's plight...
JOSH:	Like a plight of fish 'n chips, Miss!
MISS BREEZE:	Josh! ... It will help you to understand the battle, ahead of our trip to the National next month.
DANIEL:	Miss?
MISS BREEZE:	Daniel.
DANIEL:	When are we going to eat? I'm really starving.
JOSH:	Yeah and I'm tired.
MISS STEIN:	Class, listen to what Miss Breeze has to say, and we will eat very soon.
MISS BREEZE:	Thank you Miss Stein. Now. The Battle of Agincourt, 25 October 1415.
RYAN:	My brother has a sword like that at home, Miss.
MISS BREEZE:	Thank you, Ryan. Now the Battle of Agincourt was a major English victory during the Hundred Years War.
RYAN:	Only my brother's one is made of plastic, Miss. Was theirs made of plastic, Miss?
MISS BREEZE:	No Ryan.
RYAN:	What were they made of, Miss?

MISS BREEZE:	Probably steel. Now Henry was up against a vastly superior French army. Superior in number that is.
JOSH:	Miss, was there loads of blood though?
DANIEL:	Did Henry get his bollocks cut off?
MISS STEIN:	Daniel!
DANIEL:	Only asking. [*laughs*]
MISS STEIN:	Well don't.
DANIEL:	It's a valid question.
MISS BREEZE:	I can see that you boys are not interested at all in this picture.
JOSH:	Where are the nudes?
MISS BREEZE:	There are no nudes in this room, only paintings from military history.
JOSH:	I think I prefer the one next to it.
DANIEL:	Yeah.
MISS BREEZE:	Which one, Josh?
JOSH:	The one with the soldiers in that trench.
MISS BREEZE:	Ah! The First World War. We won't be looking at that till next term.
JOSH:	But that looks really good. What are they doing?
DANIEL:	Having a fag!
MISS BREEZE:	This was a famous painting depicting a temporary truce between the British and the Germans on Christmas Day December 1914.
JOSH:	That looks far more fun. [*laughs*]
MISS BREEZE:	None of it was fun, Josh. War isn't fun.
JESSICA:	I think they're both wonderful paintings Miss Breeze.
JOSH:	[*imitating her*] Ooh! wonderful paintings Miss Breeze.
JESSICA:	Shut up.
JOSH:	It's not like wars today, is it Miss?

MISS BREEZE:	No Josh.
JOSH:	Looks as if it was just them on horses playing a game, like football. Only with no ball! [*laughs*]
DANIEL:	[*laughs*] Yeah. Straight in the back of the net.
DANIEL/JOSH/RYAN:	[*chanting*] Back of the net. Back of the net. Back of the net.
MISS STEIN:	Boys, please stop that.
JESSICA:	Yes Josh, you're spoiling it for everyone.
JOSH:	Jessica, do you think you're fat, obese or morbidly obese?
JESSICA:	Just leave me alone.
MISS BREEZE:	Everybody, I think it's time to go and eat our sandwiches.
JOSH:	Looks like Jessica already ate everybody's sandwiches.
JESSICA:	You little shit!
MISS BREEZE:	Follow me please and don't get lost. Miss Stein will be taking a register again just to see if we're all together.
DANIEL:	Come on then Josh.
RYAN:	Yeah. I'm starving.
JOSH:	Wait, I've got this cool plan, right.
DANIEL:	What?
JOSH:	I've got a black felt pen on me.
RYAN:	So?
JOSH:	I'm going to sign my name on that painting.
DANIEL:	What?
RYAN:	You'll get into trouble.
JOSH:	They won't even notice.
DANIEL:	What about the security bloke.
JOSH:	He's half asleep. Shall I use the black felt tip or the red one?

DANIEL:	I dunno. I don't think you should do it. I'm off.
JOSH:	Coward.
RYAN:	Me too.
JOSH:	You're rubbish you are. Both of yers.

[JOSH *waits till the group have moved off. He gets out his felt tip, but decides to tie up his shoe lace first as a diversion. He looks about him and goes up to the painting. He takes his pen and touches the painting with the tip. Immediately an alarm goes off.*]

SECURITY GUARD: Oy, what do you think you're doing?

[*The alarm gets louder and louder, followed by another alarm with a higher pitch.* JOSH *holds his head and shuts his eyes.*]

Blackout.

JOSH: [*shocked*] I didn't do it. It was a joke. It was a joke.

SCENE 2: AGINCOURT 1415

The alarm stops and when JOSH *opens his eyes. He finds he's on a battlefield. He's in Agincourt with other soldiers marching towards the French blockade with a section shield in one hand and a sword in the other.*

JOSH:	[*screaming*] Oh help! Help!
SOLDIER 1:	Shut up.
JOSH:	What's happening? I don't understand.
SOLDIER 2:	He doesn't understand! Can't you see?
JOSH:	No. Yes. The bloke on the horse?
SOLDIER 3:	That is the King.
JOSH:	Which king?
SOLDIER 1:	I think that's treasonable. It's Henry. Are you blind?
JOSH:	No.
SOLDIER 2:	Shh! What's he saying?

HENRY V:	I will tell you all once again, so that my orders will be clear. I am splitting you into three divisions. The vanguard will be led by the Duke of York. The rear guard will be led by Lord Camoys and the rest of you will be led by myself. Now, forward men.
ALL CAST:	Yes! [screams and shouts]
HENRY V:	You must all remember the justness of this cause. I should be King of France. I have a right to the throne through my great grandfather Edward III.
ALL CAST:	Yes Majesty.
JOSH:	Hang about. Is that right though?
HENRY V:	Who said that?
SOLDIERS 1,2 & 3:	He did.
HENRY V:	Come here, boy.
JOSH:	No. You're not real. You were in that painting, and I don't know what I'm doing here. I think I threw up or fainted or something. I had a dodgy prawn sandwich!
HENRY V:	I should smite you or be damned. But on this momentous occasion I shall spare you, for you are a minor.
JOSH:	Thank Christ for that.
SOLDIER 2:	Silence.
JOSH:	Sorry.
HENRY V:	Already we are at an advantage. The French King is feeble of mind and cannot defend himself. And so we have to contend ourselves with his substitute Constable Charles d'Albret and various noblemen of the Armagnac party. But they are a bountiful army, and they must not win. For we shall all be damned to hell.
JOSH:	I wanna go home.
SOLDIER 1:	Then go.

HENRY V:	Once more unto the breach, dear friends, once more. Or close the wall up with our English dead.
JOSH:	He really said that then!
SOLDIER 3:	You have just heard the words of our Lord.
JOSH:	Yeah, but I thought it was just that Shakespeare crap.
SOLDIER 3:	Who?
JOSH:	Shakespeare. No, wait a minute, he cropped up later, didn't he?
HENRY V:	Forward.
JOSH:	I don't know what I'm supposed to do.
SOLDIER 1:	Fight.
JOSH:	But I can't. What can I do with a plastic sword and shield against an uber-sized army like the French? I can't even use a taser gun.
SOLDIER 2:	I don't know what you mean, but you must defend yourself and fight the French. Otherwise you will be run through.
SOLDIER 3:	I fear for our Longbow men, for the French have threatened to cut off two of their fingers if caught.
JOSH:	Oh shit! I can't do this.
	[JOSH *turns round and runs in the opposite direction*]
SOLDIER 1:	Where are you going?
SOLDIER:	Leave the coward to the elements. He won't get far.
JOSH:	I'm out of here. I'd rather be at the Emirates having a punch up with some Spurs' scum!

BLACK OUT

SCENE 3: DECEMBER 1914. WESTERN FRONT

All is dark except for moonlight. Soldiers are in a trench singing.

ALL CAST:	Silent night, Holy night All is calm, all is bright

Round yon virgin, mother and child
Holy infant, tender and mild
Sleep in heavenly peace.
Sleep in heavenly peace.

[JOSH *runs on stage left and falls into the trench*]

JOSH:	Oh shit. Oh my leg. Where am I?
SOLDIER 1:	Hey watch it, sonny.
SOLDIER 2:	He's a bloody Gerry. Is he alone?
SOLDIER 3:	No, he's not a Gerry. He's only a young lad. Let's have you. Who are you?
JOSH:	Oy, get off me.
SOLDIER 2:	Who are you?
JOSH:	I'm Josh and I'm lost.
SOLDIER 2:	Aren't we all, mate. Want a ciggy? I can't finish it.
JOSH:	Thanks. [*takes the cigarette, inhales it, and starts to cough and wretch*]

[*The* SOLDIERS *laugh*]

SOLDIER 2:	You're just a child.
JOSH:	No I'm not. But I'm bloody freezing.
SOLDIER 1:	Did you run away to war then? Did you think it would be a picnic?
JOSH:	Yeah. No. I thought it would be fun, you know, hiding from the enemy. But it stinks of shit in here. Where's the loo?

[*The* SOLDIERS *all laugh*]

SOLDIER 1:	First door on the right!
JOSH:	Oh my God, what's that?
SOLDIER 2:	Hah! You little school girl, you. Rats my boy, rats the size of house cats. There are millions of them, crawling up your leg, biting you when you try and snatch a couple of hours' kip.
SOLDIER 4:	Help me. Please somebody help me.

SOLDIER 2:	Poor bugger.
JOSH:	What's the matter with him?
SOLDIER 2:	Gangrene. He's one of the unlucky ones.
JOSH:	I don't know what Gangrene is.
SOLDIER 2:	I'd rather be like him over there.
JOSH:	[*panic*] But, he's… he's dead.
SOLDIER 2:	Yeah. What are you doing here anyway? Where did you come from? You're just a boy.
	[*A gas missile is thrown into the trench*]
ALL CAST:	[*shouts, screams coughing ad lib – "let's get out"*]
SOLDIER 1:	Okay. Everybody out.
SOLDIER 3:	But that's suicide.
SOLDIER 1:	[*coughs*] Would you rather be gassed to death?
SOLDIER 4:	Help me. Somebody help me.
SOLDIER 2:	[*coughs*] Poor bastard. He's as good as dead. Now boy, take this grenade in your hand, it's your only chance of getting out alive, and this gun.
JOSH:	But I don't know how to use it.
SOLDIER 2:	Bad luck.
SOLDIER 1:	Okay everybody out.

There is a great commotion as the soldiers come out of the trenches with their guns firing, throwing grenades etc. JOSH is fired at and drops down dead.

BLACK OUT

SCENE 4: ART GALLERY

JOSH *is lying on the floor of the art gallery beside the two paintings. The* SECURITY GUARD *is with him. One by one the class return.*

SECURITY GUARD: Come on son. You'll be alright.

JOSH: Where am I?

SECURITY GUARD: You're here at the art gallery.

JOSH: What happened? It's you isn't it?

SECURITY GUARD: Ay?

JOSH: You're Henry V aren't you? You was on that horse fighting the French.

SECURITY GUARD: [*winking at him*] Ssh, don't tell anyone.

[*enter* TEACHERS *and* CLASS]

MISS BREEZE: Josh, we've been looking everywhere for you. What are you doing on the floor? Get up and stop messing around, otherwise you'll have to return to the coach.

SECURITY GUARD: He'll be alright. He just had a funny turn. [*exits*]

MISS STEIN: What happened?

JOSH: I don't know.

[JOSH *looks up at the paintings*]

JOSH: Funny dream.

MISS BREEZE: Well, just take it easy. Come on, let's get you up.

[BOTH TEACHERS *help* JOSH *to his feet*]

JOSH: I just felt faint. I had a funny dream.

[*enter* DANIEL *and* RYAN]

DANIEL: You all right?

JOSH: Yeah. Course!

RYAN: Did you write on that painting?

JOSH: Nah. I didn't want to. They were brave men those soldiers. They saw a lot of death and destruction.

RYAN: That's so gay!

JOSH: Shut up. You don't understand. Anyway I was gonna put my name on it, but the ink ran out.

DANIEL: Hey, what's that on your face?

JOSH: Nothing. What?

RYAN: It looks like blood.

[RYAN *touches* JOSH's *face*]

RYAN: Yuk! It's paint.

JOSH: Paint?

RYAN: Yeah, paint! [*laughs*] So you did touch the painting after all. Yay!

JOSH: Yeah, I shook hands with Henry V before he annihilated the French. You know like Alexis Sanchez against Spurs – "back of the net"!

DANIEL/JOSH: Back of the net, back of the net!

They all walk off and as they do so, JOSH *feels in his pocket and pulls out the unexploded grenade he never threw. A look of shock crosses his face. He looks across at the* SECURITY GUARD *who looks back at him and winks.*

SECURITY GUARD: Alright?

JOSH: Yeah. Never better.

END